BUBBLE TROUBLE

TOM PERCIVAL

BLOOMSBURY
LONDON NEW DELHI NEW YORK SYDNEY

Rueben and Felix had always lived next door to each other.

They were exactly the same age,

exactly the same height
(apart from the ears),

and they were both left-handed.

They also had something else in common...

All sorts of bubbles, but mostly they liked
to blow **really**,

really...

It was their favourite thing to do,
and they always did it together.

Until one day Rueben said,
"I bet I could blow a bigger
bubble than you."

And that was how the
contest started.

pop!

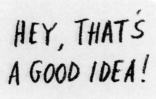

But, as their machines became more complicated, the game became less fun.

MY BUBBLES ARE THE BIGGEST!

What Rueben and Felix needed were some clear rules.

So they appointed a group of judges.

Now they would be able to determine
exactly who could blow the biggest bubbles.
At last, the competition was 'official'.

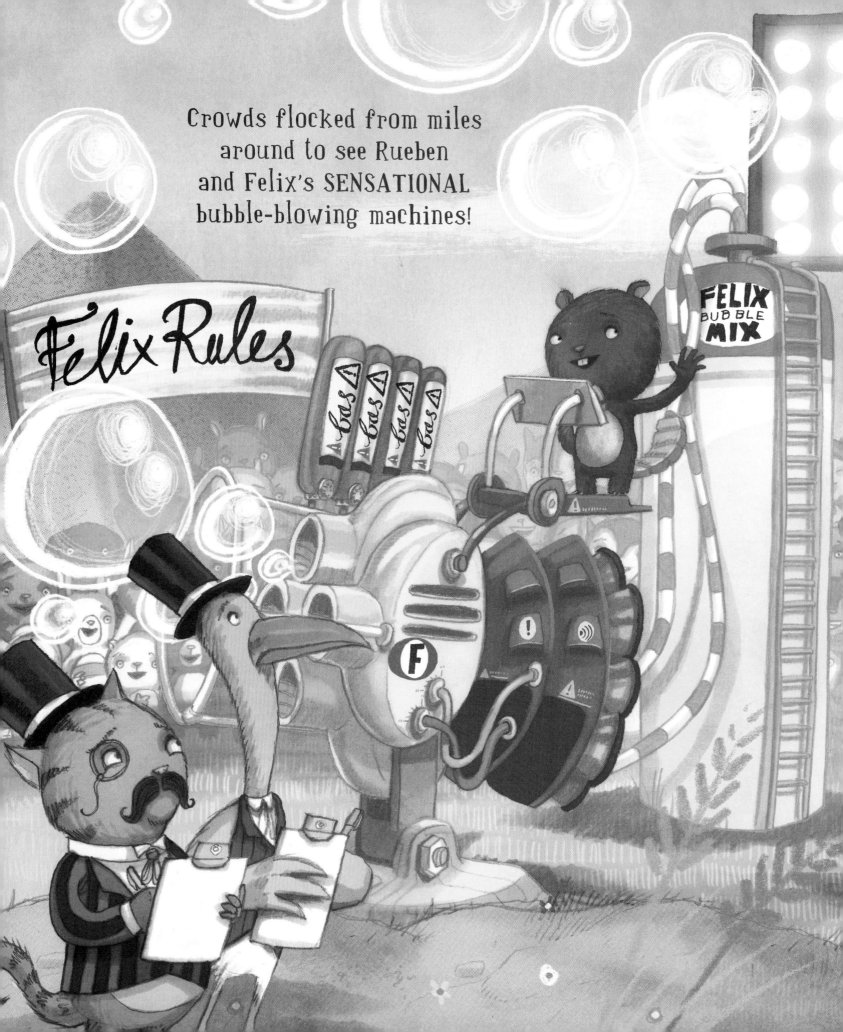

Crowds flocked from miles around to see Rueben and Felix's SENSATIONAL bubble-blowing machines!

The bubbles that they blew were huge, bright and wondrous!

Each one was **bigger** than the last.

But all Rueben and Felix
could think about was
WINNING.

Instead of just trying to blow their own bubbles,
they also came up with ingenious ways to cheat...

which didn't always work!

But Rueben and Felix
refused to give up.

The next morning
they both felt convinced that
they would finally win...

until they turned on
their bubble-blowing machines.

GRIND

CLANK

CREAK

There was
a **clanking**
and a **creaking**,
a **grinding**
and a **groaning**.

Followed by a
VERY LOUD...

Now Rueben and Felix realised just how silly they had been.
They didn't need all that complicated machinery...

all they needed was a little bit of help.

BUBBLES

So they gathered everyone together.

And on a count of three - 1 , 2 , 3
- they all began to blow.

Slowly, the bubble grew.
And it
grew...
and it
grew...
and it
grew...

until...

together they had
blown the **biggest bubble**
in the world!

Everything was back as it should be.
Rueben and Felix were best friends again.

YIPPEE!

And *nothing* was EVER
going to change that.

THE NEWSPAPER R R

FEATURES

GET BRIGHTER EYES

MAKE YOUR TAIL BUSHIER

BEAR'S TOILET IN WOODS CONDEMNED

BEST FRIENDS BLOW BRILLIANT BUBBLE

MASKED HERO SAVES THE DAY

Until Felix said...

"I bet I can **jump** higher than you..."

THIS BOOK IS FOR AMELIE

Bloomsbury Publishing, London, New Delhi, New York and Sydney

First published in Great Britain in 2014 by Bloomsbury Publishing Plc
50 Bedford Square, London, WC1B 3DP

Text and illustrations copyright © Tom Percival 2014
The moral rights of the author/illustrator have been asserted

A CIP catalogue record for this book is available from the British Library

ISBN 978 1 4088 3876 1 (HB)
ISBN 978 1 4088 3877 8 (PB)
ISBN 978 1 4088 3875 4 (eBook)

Printed in China by Leo Paper Products, Heshan, Guangdong

1 3 5 7 9 10 8 6 4 2

www.bloomsbury.com

BLOOMSBURY is a registered trademark of Bloomsbury Publishing Plc